First published in the United States 1993 by
Dial Books for Young Readers
A Division of Penguin Books USA Inc.
375 Hudson Street
New York, New York 10014

Published in Great Britain 1992 by
The Bodley Head Children's Books,
an imprint of The Random Century Group Ltd
Copyright © 1992 by Bodel Rikys
All rights reserved
Printed in Singapore
First Edition
1 3 5 7 9 10 8 6 4 2

Library of Congress Cataloging in Publication Data
Rikys, Bodel. Red bear's fun with shapes / Bodel Rikys.—U.S. ed.
p.   cm.
Summary: Red Bear explores the shapes in his world,
both inside and outdoors.
ISBN 0-8037-1317-7
1. Geometry—Juvenile literature. [1. Shape.] I. Title.
QA445.5.R55   1993   516'.15—dc20   91-46997   CIP   AC

The full-color artwork was prepared using oil pastels,
with the line drawn in brush and India ink.

# Red Bear's
## Fun With Shapes

## Bodel Rikys

New York  Dial Books for Young Readers

**oval**

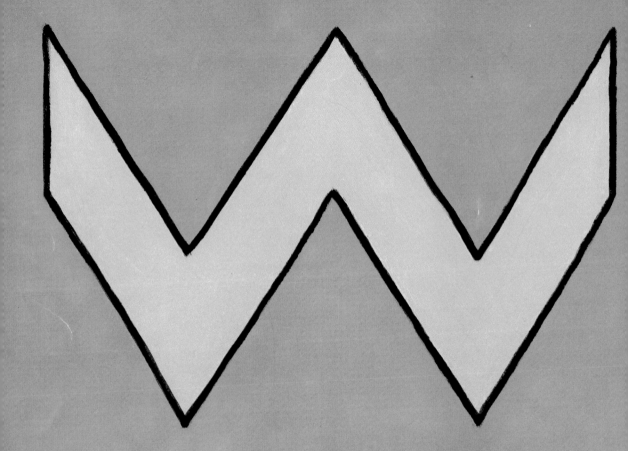

**zigzag**

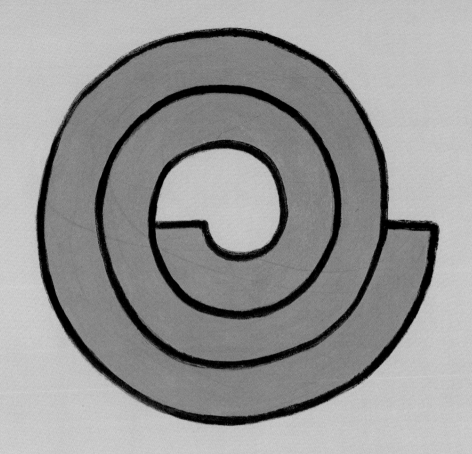

spiral

# square

triangle

circle

# diamond

**semicircle**

# rectangle

**star**

# crescent